# THIRD GRADE PET

# THIRD GRADE PET

## by Judy Cox

### illustrated by Cynthia Fisher

*Holiday House / New York*

*Text copyright © 1998 by Judy Cox*
*Illustrations copyright © 1998 by Cynthia Fisher*
**ALL RIGHTS RESERVED**
*Printed in the United States of America*
**FIRST EDITION**

Library of Congress Cataloging-in-Publication Data
Cox, Judy.
Third grade pet / by Judy Cox; illustrated by Cynthia Fisher.
— 1st ed.
p.    cm.
Summary: Fearing for the safety of the third grade's class pet,
Cheese the rat, Rosemary takes him home in her backpack and creates
chaos in the household.
ISBN 0–8234–1379–9
[1. Rats—Fiction.   2. Pets—Fiction.   3. Schools—Fiction.]
I. Fisher, Cynthia, ill.   II. Title.
PZ8.3.C8375Th        1998        98–6896        CIP        AC
[Fic]—DC21

*To the kids in Mrs. Cox's class*

# Contents

1.  Rats Are Yucky!                                    1
2.  Perky Pets for Perky People                        8
3.  "I Can't Believe It!"                             15
4.  Rat Keepers                                       23
5.  The Loveliest Rat in the World                    29
6.  Rat Rescue!                                       35
7.  Close Calls                                       43
8.  The Orthodontist                                  51
9.  Spot Wants Mousey!                                59
10. Spot Gots Mousey!                                 66
11. No Place for a Rat                                73
12. Rosemary and Cheese, Too                          79
    Rosemary's Rat Care Tips                          88

# THIRD GRADE PET

# 1

# *Rats Are Yucky!*

"Hey! Metal mouth!"

Brian Jones pulled Rosemary's ponytail. He slid into the desk in front of her.

"Don't call me that!" Rosemary snapped.

Brian lifted his sunglasses. He peered underneath and grinned.

"Okey-dokey, tinsel teeth," he said.

"Just ignore him," said Megan.

Megan was Rosemary's best friend. They sat together at lunch. They played horses together at recess. They walked to and from school together.

*Clap, clap, clap-clap-clap!*

Mr. Wilder called his third-graders to attention. Rosemary stopped writing. "I have a surprise for the class," said Mr. Wilder. "Please meet me on the rug. Brian, put the scissors down. Now."

"A surprise!" whispered Rosemary. "What do you think it is?"

"I hope it's something edible," said Megan.

Rosemary ran her tongue over her braces. "But not a sticky food." Last week's extra-credit word had been *edible,* and Mr. Wilder had given them dried apricots to eat. It had taken Rosemary a long time to pick the sticky bits off her braces.

Rosemary and Megan put their papers inside their folders and sat on the rug. Mr. Wilder was smiling.

"So, where's the surprise?" said Tom.

"Patience," said Mr. Wilder. "We need everyone. Brian, we're waiting for you."

"First is worst! Second is best! Third is the one in the ballerina dress!" Brian yelled.

He skidded to the rug as though sliding into first base. He still had on his sunglasses. They went with the red aloha shirt he always wore,

and the baggy shorts. Rain or shine, Brian dressed as if he were on vacation.

"I've decided we should get a class pet," said Mr. Wilder. "A class pet will be useful for observing the habits of animals firsthand. It will promote compassion among you young renegades, and perhaps teach you some responsibility." He smiled. "And it will be fun."

A pet! thought Rosemary. What would it be? In kindergarten they'd had a guinea pig. But Rosemary hadn't liked it. It had smelled funny.

Bette raised her hand. "Can we get a boa constrictor?"

"No!" shouted Anthony. "Let's get a turtle!"

"How about a talking parrot?" said Matt. "My aunt has one. It can say 'Hello' and 'Chill out'!"

"I think hamsters make the best pets," said Rene. "Or a guinea pig. No, I've got it! We should get a rat!"

"Yeah!" said Brian. "A rat! I used to have rats! They're cool!"

Rosemary shivered. Not a rat, please not a rat. Just the thought of that long, bare rat tail gave her the creeps.

"We'll need a cage," said Brian.

"Food!"

"Water!"

"Toys!"

"A ball it can go in! Yeah, a plastic ball like on TV!"

"That won't be much use to a snake," said Anthony.

"We're getting a rat!" shouted Brian.

Mr. Wilder laughed.

"Whoa, there," he said. "Before we decide what animal to buy, we need to do some research."

The kids groaned.

"On Friday, we'll take a field trip to the pet store to find out how much each pet would cost, what it would eat, and what kind of cage we'd need to buy. Then we'll decide. Questions? Matt?"

"How much money can we spend?" asked Matt.

"We have fifty dollars left in our class fund," said Mr. Wilder. "We can spend all of it or part of it. Now, back to your seats. Get out your journals. Write about an animal you'd like to have for a pet."

Back at her desk, Rosemary sucked on the end of her pencil. She didn't know much about pets. She didn't have a pet, not even a goldfish. Mom said their house was too small, money was too tight, and pets were too messy. Rosemary thought Mom was probably right. She usually was. But it might be nice to have something.

"What are you writing about?" she whispered to Megan.

"Horses," Megan whispered back. "I want a palomino horse."

Of course. They both wanted horses. But did a horse count as a pet?

Brian turned around. He had a pencil sticking out of each nostril. "I'm writing about rats!" he said.

Rosemary started writing. Any pet would do.

So long as it wasn't a rat.

# 2

# *Perky Pets for Perky People*

"What pet do you think we'll buy?" Megan asked Rosemary.

It was Friday. The class was traveling downtown on the bus to visit the pet store.

"Well, it won't be a horse," said Rosemary. "Horses are too big. They smell too much and eat too much hay. Besides, they don't sell horses at pet stores."

Megan sighed. "I know. I never really thought we would get a horse. But I hope we don't get a snake."

Rosemary shook her head. "A snake would be okay with me, as long as I don't have to hold it. I hope we don't get a rat!" She shivered.

"Why not?"

"Rats are dirty. They live in sewers. They have fleas that give you diseases. They bite. Rats are my worst nightmare."

"Then I'll hope we don't get a rat, too," said Megan.

Rosemary gave her a smile. Megan was a good friend.

Brian turned around in his seat. He was wearing his sunglasses even though it was raining. He hunched his shoulders and waved his fingers at Rosemary.

"Ooo!" he whispered. "You dirty rat! I'm gonna get ya! You dirty rat!"

Rosemary glared at him. Megan touched her arm. "Just ignore him," she said.

The bus pulled up in front of the pet store. The sign said:

PERKY PET STORE:

PERKY PETS FOR PERKY PEOPLE

Mr. Wilder led his class inside. "I expect you to be on your best behavior," he warned.

Matt ran over to the parrot cage.

"Hello! Hello there! Hello there!" screeched the parrot.

"A talking parrot!" Matt exclaimed. "Like Aunt Tilda's!"

The parrot was green with a big black beak. Rosemary looked at the price tag.

"No way, José," she told Matt. "That bird costs fifteen hundred dollars. And that doesn't include the birdcage."

"I think a talking parrot would interrupt too much, anyway," said Mr. Wilder. He laughed. "And if there's one thing I don't need, it's more interruptions in class!"

"Where are the boas?" asked Bette.

The pet-store clerk came over. She said her name was Molly. She led them to the back of the store. The snakes were in lighted terrariums on shelves. There were chameleons and iguanas, too.

"If you want a snake, you'll need a terrarium and a light. Snakes have to be kept warm all the time," said Molly.

Anthony got out his calculator. A terrarium with a light cost $80. A boa was $250. Way too much money.

"How about a hedgehog?" asked Rene. "Hedgehogs are cute. They are quiet. They don't need a light to keep them warm. We could name her Mrs. Tiggy-winkle."

Rene was a Beatrix Potter fan.

"We could name him Sonic!" said Brian, who wasn't.

But the hedgehogs were too much money as well. A single hedgehog cost $150.

"That's three times what we have to spend," Brian said sadly. "And no cage."

"Perhaps you should get a hermit crab," said Molly. "It's only six dollars. I could sell you a fishbowl and some gravel for ten. Throw in some food."

Molly led the way to the hermit crabs. The class followed single file, down the narrow aisle. Brian was behind Rosemary. He made his fingers into pincers.

"I'm a crab!" he said, pinching her.

"Pizza breath!" spat Rosemary.

She turned and caught Mr. Wilder's warning look.

Before they reached the hermit crabs, the class passed a shelf of small-animal cages.

"Ooh! Mice!" cried Rene. She bent down to peek into a cage of tiny white mice.

"Gerbils!" said Anthony.

"Hamsters!" shouted Tom.

"Guinea pigs!" yelled Bette.

"No! Guys, look here!" said Brian. *"Rats!"*

The class pressed eagerly around a glass cage filled with rats. Only Rosemary stood back.

A sleek black rat sat up to wash his face. Three white rats curled up on top of one another. A gray-and-white rat stood on his hind legs, his pink paws pressed to the glass.

"Oh, they're so cute! Let's get a rat," said Bette.

"I want the black one!" shouted Tom.

"The white one! We can name her Snowy."

"No way! What kind of name is that for a rat? We need a tough name, like . . . like . . . Mario!" said Brian.

We don't need a rat at all, thought Rosemary. Please no. Not a dirty, flea-bitten rat. Anything but a rat.

# 3

# "I Can't Believe It!"

"I can't believe we got a *rat*," Rosemary said to Megan as they walked home from school.

Megan sighed. "I know. Your worst nightmare." She swung her backpack. "But don't you think he's kind of cute? Just a little bit?"

Rosemary thought about the new class pet. Mr. Wilder had put the cage on the science table. The rat was smaller than she had expected. He had white fur and a gray head. His eyes were black and shiny.

But even this rat had a long, bare tail. And when he gnawed the carrot Mr. Wilder had given him, Rosemary had clearly seen his very sharp front teeth. Two on top, two on bottom. Like fangs. Rosemary shivered.

"No, I don't. I told you. I don't like rats. I dream about them sometimes. Hordes of creepy rats, swarming out at midnight, gnawing everything in their path . . ." She waved her fingers under her chin.

Megan laughed. "You've been watching too many horror movies, Rosie! Our rat is just a little gray-hooded rat."

"But, Megan! What about his tail? His teeth? Those long claws?" Rosemary frowned.

"Those aren't claws," said Megan. "Those are his toes. His claws are really tiny. You'll see on Monday, when Mr. Wilder shows us how to hold him. And," she added, "on Monday Mr. Wilder will pick a rat keeper."

"Well, it won't be me," said Rosemary.

"Railroad tracks!" Brian streaked past them and skidded to a stop. "Beggin' Megan!"

"Ignore him," whispered Megan. "He just

16

wants attention."

"I should be the rat keeper," said Brian. "I used to have rats at home."

"I'll bet," said Rosemary. "Under your bed, probably."

Brian lifted his sunglasses and looked at her.

"No. *Pet* rats. In a cage. I had a boy rat and a girl rat and they had babies. Lots of babies. But they got sick and died."

He kicked his backpack down the sidewalk. "Look out below!" he shouted, running after it.

"So I should be rat keeper first," he called over his shoulder. "Because I *know* about rats!"

"He *is* a rat," giggled Megan. "A sewer rat!"

Rosemary rolled her eyes. "Just so long as *I* never have to do it."

She waved good-bye as Megan galloped up the steps to her front door.

Rosemary raced two houses down to her own house. She pounded up the porch stairs and flung open the door.

"Wo! Wo!" cried her little brother.

He toddled over and held up his arms.

"Hi ya, Spot," said Rosemary.

She picked him up and swung him around. His real name was Spofford, after their grandpa Spofford Robinson, but Rosemary called him Spot. "It's what he does best," she once told her parents. "He leaves spots on the carpet, spots on my toys, spots on my books."

"How was your field trip, sweetie?" asked Mom.

Rosemary grabbed a handful of baby carrots from the fridge. "Awful. The class bought a rat! A *rat*!"

"Yuck." Mom shivered. "Rosemary, I have an important fax coming in. Please keep an eye on Spofford until Dad gets home." She headed for her office.

Rosemary sighed. Mom wrote newsletters for a real estate company. Sometimes it was great to have a mom who worked at home. At least Rosemary didn't have to go to a sitter after school, like Brian. But Mom's office was strictly off limits unless Rosemary or Spot was bleeding. Sometimes Rosemary just felt like an unpaid baby-sitter.

She gave Spot a graham cracker. He stuffed it down the front of his overalls. Spot always did that. He thought he was putting it in his pocket. When Mom undressed him to bathe him, he was always covered with graham-cracker crumbs. Rosemary wondered how he could stand the itching.

"Mo," Spot demanded.

Rosemary gave him another cracker, which he crammed into his mouth. He gave her a sticky grin, his baby teeth coated with crumbs.

"Pay me!"

That was Spot's way of saying "Play with me." Not everyone could understand Spot. But Rosemary always knew what he meant.

"Come on." She sighed again and took him by the hand. "Let's go see my horses."


Rosemary's room looked like a stable. Drawings of horses were tacked on the walls. Statues of horses, ponies, mares, and stallions pranced across her bookshelf. Pinned to her bulletin board were homemade ribbons. Blue ones. First Place in her pretend horse shows.

Spot loved Rosemary's room.

"Pony," he sighed, reaching for Rosemary's plastic pony statue.

It was her favorite, a white one with gray spots. Rosemary wiped Spot's hands before giving it to him. He stroked it happily while she carefully dusted each of her other horses.

"Well, Spotty," she told her brother, "at least I won't have to have anything to do with the rat. Not even look at him."

She certainly hoped not.

# 4

# *Rat Keepers*

*Clap, clap, clap-clap-clap!*

On Monday, Mr. Wilder called the class up to the rug. Rosemary went as slowly as she could. She knew Mr. Wilder was going to talk about the rat.

"We need to vote on a name for our class rat," said Mr. Wilder. "Then I'll show everyone how to hold him and how to care for him. Each week, two students will be in charge of feeding him and cleaning his cage."

"Rat keepers!" yelled Brian.

Mr. Wilder laughed. "Exactly. Now, any ideas for names?"

Rosemary sat on her hands. No way was she naming a rat. Maybe she wouldn't get called on.

"Snowy!" called Rene.

"Nah, that's babyish," said Anthony. "Let's call him Tiger."

"Ben!" shouted Tom.

"Tom!" shouted Ben.

"Brian!" shouted Brian.

Mr. Wilder laughed. "I think it would be pretty confusing to have two Bens or Toms or Brians in this class. One of each is quite enough!"

"Robot!" said Bette.

"Cutie pie!"

"Snarly!"

The names came thick and fast. Rosemary watched Mr. Wilder write them on the board. Those aren't good names for rats, she thought. No one is as good at naming as I am. She glanced at the rat in the tank. He was sitting up on his hind feet, washing his whiskers.

Once she'd fed a squirrel in the park. He sat up on his hind legs just like that. Rosemary named

him Nuts. But Nuts wasn't a good rat name. Cheese, thought Rosemary. That's his name.

Without meaning to, Rosemary shouted it out. "*Cheese!* Mr. Wilder! *Cheese!*"

"Yeah!" yelled Brian. "Cheese. That's a great name! Let's name him Cheese."

The class voted. Everyone agreed. The rat's name was Cheese.

"Good idea, Rosemary," said Mr. Wilder.

Mr. Wilder took the screen off the top of the glass tank. He set it on the floor.

"Gently," he told the class.

He slid his hand under Cheese. "The trick is not to scare him. Animals need to be treated with respect and kindness."

Mr. Wilder lifted Cheese and cradled him against his chest. Cheese ran up his arm. He buried his head in the curve of Mr. Wilder's elbow. Only his tail showed. The class laughed.

"Remember, if you scare him or hurt him, he might bite. Never squeeze him, either. It could bruise his internal organs."

Mr. Wilder stroked Cheese with one finger. "Who wants a turn?"

Everyone except Rosemary waved a hand, even Megan. Rosemary watched Cheese through narrowed eyes. What if he bit? What if he went to the bathroom on her?

Mr. Wilder gave Cheese to Bette. He showed the class how to fill his bowl with food and check his water. He told them how to clean the tank and fill it with fresh fir shavings.

"Each week, I'll pick two students to take care of Cheese," Mr. Wilder said. "Rats, like kids, need exercise and play, so it will be the rat keepers' job to make friends with Cheese. Let's see."

He looked around the room. "We'll start with Brian, because he's had pet rats."

Brian grinned.

"And Rosemary," continued Mr. Wilder, "because she thought up the name."

Rosemary's blood turned to ice. Rat keeper. For a whole week. It was like a nightmare come true.


All afternoon, Rosemary stared at the rat. It was as if the rat were a magnet and her eyes were iron filings. Brian plopped down in the seat next to her.

"This is great, huh? First rat keepers. I can't wait until choice time today when we can hold him. I'll go first, okay?"

Rosemary nodded.

Knowing Brian, he wouldn't even give her a chance to hold Cheese. And that was okay with her.

# 5

# *The Loveliest Rat in the World*

It was Tuesday. Brian was sick. Rosemary was the rat keeper. The only rat keeper for the whole day. "Lucky stiff," said Tom. All the kids thought she was lucky. Only Megan knew how she truly felt.

"If you really are too scared to hold Cheese, why don't you tell Mr. Wilder?" she asked. "He won't make you. He's nice. He let me do PE in my socks the day I forgot my gym shoes."

But Rosemary didn't want to tell Mr. Wilder. She couldn't explain it. She didn't like rats. She *hated* rats. But Cheese was different.

All morning, she watched Cheese. All during reading and computer, right through math and spelling. His little black eyes. His little pink ears. His long tail. Megan was right. He was kind of cute. Not like a regular rat.

But that didn't mean she wanted to touch him.

"Closer, Rosemary," said Mr. Wilder. "Let him smell your fingers. Let him get used to you so he's not startled when you pick him up."

Cheese was curled up in a nest of fir shavings. Rosemary held her breath. She dangled her fingers in the tank.

She shivered. She inched her fingers closer. Cheese's eyes sprang open. His whiskers quivered. Rosemary watched his nose wiggle as he sniffed her fingers. It didn't hurt at all.

"You can pet him," Mr. Wilder said.

Rosemary stroked Cheese with one finger. His fur was soft and warm.

"Now, slide your hand under his belly and lift him up," Mr. Wilder said.

Rosemary took a deep breath. Slowly, she slipped her hand under Cheese. She brought

him up to her chest. Cheese buried his head in
the curve of her elbow.

Goose bumps rose on her skin. "It's scratchy," she said.

"Those are his claws," said Mr. Wilder.

Rosemary shivered again. She forced herself to look at the rat. He had tiny pink paws like little hands. His claws were nearly invisible, small and clear. They didn't really *hurt*.

Rosemary sat down cross-legged on the rug. She put Cheese on the floor between her legs. Mr. Wilder said it was her job to get Cheese used to people.

Cheese climbed up on her knee. His pink tail wasn't bare after all. It was covered with little white hairs. Rosemary touched his tail with one finger. It was warm. Cheese, startled, hunched up in a little ball. All the time, his beady, bright eyes were watching her.

Mr. Wilder had told the class that rats don't see very well. They depend on their ears and noses. Cheese's ears were pink and gray. They were as soft as rose petals.

"Cheese," whispered Rosemary.

His ears came forward to catch every sound. He climbed her leg. Then he suddenly burrowed inside the sleeve of her sweater and disappeared up her arm.

Rosemary froze. Cheese was inside her sleeve. Only his long pink tail showed. She could feel him crawling up her arm. Where will he go? Her breath came fast. Will he bite me? How can I get him out? Should I tell Mr. Wilder? Cheese was completely hidden. Now, not even his tail showed.

Cheese did not bite. After a while, Rosemary realized that his body was warm and furry inside her sweater. She opened her cuff with her other hand. Cheese poked his nose out. She relaxed. Cheese came out.

Rosemary scooped him up and put him back in his tank. She gave him a carrot. He sniffed her fingers as if to say thank you.

Rosemary pressed her nose against the side of his tank to watch. Cheese's shiny black eyes watched her, too. He turned the carrot around in his paws as he nibbled. He was not dirty. He was not yucky or mean or flea bitten.

There was no doubt about it. Cheese was the loveliest rat in the world.

# 6

# *Rat Rescue!*

"Hi ya, scissor lips!" Brian tugged Rosemary's ponytail.

He slid into his seat. It was Wednesday. Brian wore his superpower sunglasses and his red shirt with the palm trees. It was thirty-nine degrees outside. Brian looked like summer.

"Just ignore him," whispered Megan.

Rosemary was not happy to see him.

"He'll want to hog Cheese," she told Megan. "And he doesn't know a thing about rats."

"But he used to have rats. He told us."

Rosemary shook her head. "And look what happened to them! I've been reading up on rats. They're smart. They need food and water and exercise and love—like people do. I don't think Brian is a good rat keeper."

"Oh, Rosemary, you worry too much. Cheese will be okay."

But Rosemary wasn't sure.

At choice time, Brian grabbed Cheese by the tail.

"No!" said Rosemary. "You'll hurt him!"

Brian lifted his sunglasses to stare at her.

"They like it," he said. "I've had rats, so I know."

He reached into the tank again, but Rosemary was too quick. She put her hand down, palm up. Cheese sniffed. His whiskers twitched. He scurried onto her hand.

Rosemary was charmed. Cheese knew her! He wanted to sit with her!

"See," said Rosemary. "That's the way to pick him up."

Brian's mouth turned down at the corners. He sat on the rug beside Rosemary.

"It's my turn now," he said. "You had him all day yesterday. I should get him all day today."

But Cheese would not stay with Brian. Every time Rosemary handed Cheese to Brian, Cheese ran back into her lap. He scurried up her arm and sat on her shoulder. His whiskers tickled her cheek. He hid under her ponytail. Brian scowled.

"It's my turn!" he said.

He grabbed Cheese around the tummy and yanked him away.

"Don't do that! You might kill him!" scolded Rosemary.

Her heart pounded. Was Cheese hurt?

Cheese wriggled free. He leaped into Rosemary's lap.

Brian frowned.

"Cheater!" he said. "It was my turn!"

"I can't help it if Cheese likes me better!"

"I'm telling Mr. Wilder!" Brian stormed off.

"There, there," she whispered.

She stroked Cheese's back. He trembled.

In a minute, Brian was back. He looked smug.

"You can have him," he said. "Mr. Wilder said if it's okay with my mom, I can take him home with me tomorrow. I can keep him all day Friday, and for the whole weekend. So ha-ha, Rosie!"

Rosemary listened with a sinking heart. She carefully lowered Cheese back into his tank.

She went to find her friend. "Megan! Something awful happened! Brian gets to keep Cheese for the whole weekend!"

Megan looked up from the palomino horse she was drawing.

"So?" she asked. "I thought you didn't like rats."

Rosemary stamped her foot. "Don't you understand? Cheese is different! He's not like a regular rat. He's little and soft. And he knows me. He'll be in danger at Brian's house! Brian brags about all the rats he once had, and where are they now? Dead, that's where!"

Megan shook her head. "That's awful," she said. "But Cheese'll be okay. Anyway, we can always buy a new rat."

Rosemary's eyes widened. Megan didn't understand at all. Cheese wasn't just any rat; he was Cheese! He should never go to Brian's house. She couldn't, wouldn't let it happen. Something had to be done.

❖ ❖ ❖

At choice time on Thursday, Rosemary held out a carrot. Cheese sat up and took it between his paws. Brian reached out to grab him.

"Cat bait," laughed Brian. "My cat could gulp you down in one bite."

Rosemary grew hot and cold.

*Clap, clap, clap-clap-clap!*

"Time to go home," said Mr. Wilder. "Get your backpacks and line up."

The noise startled Cheese. He ran inside the sleeve of Rosemary's sweater and hid.

Brian smirked. "My baby-sitter is coming to pick me up. I get to take Cheese home today. I have to wait here for her."

He went to get his backpack.

Rosemary pulled up her cuff to look at Cheese. His nose wiggled. She couldn't let him go with Brian. Especially not after he'd called him cat bait.

She rolled her sleeve back down. Cheese was completely hidden. Rosemary snatched up her backpack. She slipped through the bus line and out the door. She didn't even wait for Megan.

"Rosemary!" Mr. Wilder called.

The back of Rosemary's neck prickled. Mr. Wilder must have noticed the empty cage. She was caught!

"Rosemary! Don't forget your homework." Mr. Wilder held out her math book.

She took it. He smiled. She turned and ran out the door. She was safe. Nobody saw. Nobody knew.

# 7

# *Close Calls*

"Rosie! Wait up!" Megan called.

Rosemary didn't stop. She'd explain to Megan later. The important thing was to get Cheese home.

She dashed through the crowded hallway. She pushed the door open and ran outside.

"Walk, please!" shouted a teacher on bus duty.

But Rosemary didn't slow down. She hurried across the street, past the crossing guards. She looked behind her. No Mr. Wilder. No Brian.

So far, so good.

She could feel Cheese under her sweater. His whiskers tickled. Or was that the pricking of his tiny claws? She pulled her sweater loose and hoped no one would notice the lump he made.

She rounded the corner. No other kids were walking home yet. She'd done it! She'd rescued Cheese from a fate worse than death: Brian!

*Woof! Woof!*

A dog streaked out of a side yard.

Rosemary jumped.

The dog jerked to a stop just in front of her legs. There was a chain around his neck. He strained against it, barking and growling.

Rosemary ran past. Could he smell Cheese?

Cheese dug into her arm with his claws. Her arm felt damp. Had Cheese gone to the bathroom? She couldn't blame him. He must be scared.

She needed to go to the bathroom, too. She always felt like that when she was scared.

Only three more blocks to go. At the corner, Mrs. Enderby came outside. She was holding Snookums, her Persian cat.

"Rosemary! Rosie, dear!" she called. "Did you hear about Snookums's poor ear?"

Mrs. Enderby stood right in front of Rosemary. She was a very big lady. Her cat was big, too. Rosemary couldn't get by. Snookums wriggled in Mrs. Enderby's arms. He had mean yellow eyes.

Snookums could certainly smell Cheese.

"What's gotten into him?" asked Mrs. Enderby. "I can't hold him."

Snookums's tail twitched. He struggled to get out of Mrs. Enderby's arms.

"I've got to go, Mrs. Enderby," said Rosemary. "I'll see you later."

Rosemary dashed off. Two more blocks and she'd be home safe.

A car pulled up to the curb next to her. The door swung open.

*"Rosemary Robinson!* What are you doing?"

Rosemary jumped a mile. It was Mom. Cheese crawled under Rosemary's sweater. Rosemary folded her arms across her chest. Mom didn't notice.

"Did you forget your orthodontist appointment? You knew I was picking you up after school! Mr. Wilder said you didn't even wait."

Mom's voice was sharp. She seemed angry.

Rosemary slid into the backseat. Spot was in his car seat.

"Sorry, Mom. I forgot."

Mom started the car up. "Now we'll be late."

Spot banged on the seat when he saw Rosemary.

"Go home! Go home!"

"Not yet, Spofford, dear," said Mom. "First the orthodontist."

Rosemary held Cheese under her sweater. She had to hide him. If Mom saw him . . . Boy, would she catch it!

She looked at Mom in the rearview mirror. Mom's eyes had that busy look grown-ups get when they are driving. This was her chance to hide Cheese.

She slid her hand under her sweater. Spot turned to watch. Rosemary scooped Cheese up and pulled him out. He didn't want to come. His

claws raked down her arm. She pulled her
backpack open and pushed Cheese inside. She
looked up. Spot was staring at her.

"Wo gots mousey," he told Mom.

"That's nice, dear," said Mom. She signaled
for a left turn.

Rosemary put her finger to her lips. "Shhh!"

"Mousey!" Spot whispered. "Shhh!"

Mom gave Rosemary a look in the mirror.

"What are you two up to?" She didn't sound angry anymore.

*Scritch. Scritch. Scritch-scratch.*

Rosemary listened in horror. Cheese was gnawing on her lunch box inside her backpack.

"What's that?" asked Mom.

In the mirror, Rosemary saw her frown.

"What's what?"

"That noise. That scratching noise." Mom sighed. "I guess I'll have to take the car in to the shop again. The mechanic laughs at me when I tell him the car sounds funny. I hate it! What would you say this sounds like?"

"Mousey!" crowed Spot.

"A mouse nibbling on plastic?" Mom signaled for a turn. "No, too loud. Mice are quiet."

"Wo gots mousey," added Spot.

Rosemary had to keep Spot from telling.

"Knock-knock!" she said.

Spot giggled. He loved knock-knock jokes. Nobody knew why. He didn't get the jokes.

Mom played along.

"Who's there?"

"Banana," said Rosemary.

"Banana who?" said Mom.

Spot laughed. It covered up the sound of Cheese's gnawing.

"Knock-knock."

"Who's there?"

"Banana."

"Banana who?" Mom said patiently.

Rosemary knew Mom had heard the joke before. In fact, Rosemary had told it to her before. Several times.

"Knock-knock."

"Who's there?"

"Orange."

Spot pounded on his seat.

"Orange who?" Mom sighed.

"Orange you glad I didn't say banana?"

Spot roared with delight. Mom pulled in front of Dr. Gibbon's office. Rosemary heaved a sigh of relief.

# 8

# *The Orthodontist*

Mom waited in the car with Spot. Rosemary opened the door to Dr. Gibbon's office. The lady at the desk fixed Rosemary with a stern look.

"Late again, Ms. Robinson," she said. "Tsk, tsk, tsk."

Rosemary blushed.

"Leave your sweater and backpack on the coat rack. Mustn't keep Doctor waiting."

Rosemary felt cold when she realized that she still held her backpack. Why hadn't she left it in the car? She remembered Spot. No, Cheese would be safer with her. But she couldn't leave her backpack in the waiting room.

She hung up her sweater and held her backpack behind her. She hoped the office lady wouldn't see it. With one hand, she opened the door to the other room.

Dr. Gibbon was waiting for her.

"Good afternoon, Rosemary," he said, smiling.

Dr. Gibbon was a handsome man. His blond hair was shiny. His teeth were big and white and beautiful. Rosemary thought they looked like sugar cubes. Rosemary smiled back.

Rosemary climbed into the chair. She set her backpack carefully on her lap. What was Cheese doing now? Could he breathe okay? Dr. Gibbon clipped a bib around her neck. Then he whisked her backpack off her lap and set it on a stool.

"No!" cried Rosemary.

"It'll be fine there, Rosemary. Come on. Let's get started."

Dr. Gibbon pulled on rubber gloves and a face mask. He started to tighten the wires on Rosemary's braces.

Rosemary lay on the chair. Her mouth hung open. It was full of Dr. Gibbon's fingers. Dr. Gibbon curled the wires with pliers. It hurt. Rosemary could hear Cheese scratching inside the backpack.

Suddenly Dr. Gibbon dropped his tray. Dental tools, cotton, floss, and brushes clattered to the floor.

"A mouse! It's a mouse!" he yelled. "I hate mice!"

Rosemary gasped. She sat up suddenly. Her head hit Dr. Gibbon's chin. She scrambled off the chair. She couldn't see Cheese anywhere. Dr. Gibbon was still yelling.

"Mrs. Watson! Mrs. Watson! Get in here! Call the exterminator! Bring a trap!"

The grouchy office lady ran in.

Rosemary spotted Cheese on the stool. He must have crawled out of her backpack. His whiskers quivered like violin strings. Rosemary sprang to the stool to grab him. But Cheese was too quick. He leaped off the stool and scurried across the floor.

Dr. Gibbon dashed out of the room, leaving Rosemary alone with the grouchy lady. Cheese ducked under the chair. Rosemary dived after him.

"Come here, Cheese," coaxed Rosemary.

She crept up on him. She almost had him.

The door banged open. Dr. Gibbon strode in, holding a broom.

"Hit him with this, Mrs. Watson," he said, handing the broom to the grouchy lady.

Startled, Cheese darted under the supply cabinet.

"Where is it?" demanded Dr. Gibbon.

"*What* is it?" demanded Mrs. Watson.

"It's okay, it's okay," said Rosemary.

She got down on her hands and knees to peer under the cupboard.

"Don't hurt him. It's just my rat. He must have gotten out of my backpack."

She couldn't see Cheese. She slid her hand under the cupboard. Cheese ran up her arm to her shoulder.

"Got him!" said Rosemary.

But Cheese didn't stop. He leaped from her shoulder to the windowsill. He swarmed up the cord of the miniblind to the top of the window. There he clung, his tail wrapped around the blind. He peered down at them with bright eyes. His body shook. His whiskers twitched.

"Oh no," moaned Rosemary. "How will I get him now?"

Dr. Gibbon glared at Rosemary.

"I want that rodent out of this office. It's unsanitary."

"Here, Cheese!" called Rosemary.

She turned to Dr. Gibbon. "He'll come to me. He *knows* me."

"Well, *I'm* not touching him," said Dr. Gibbon.

Mrs. Watson was made of sterner stuff. She climbed on the stool and scooped up Cheese, holding him gently around his tummy. She handed him down to Rosemary.

Then she smiled.

"My granddaughter has rats," she said.

She didn't look grouchy now. Rosemary held Cheese. She stroked him with her finger until he

calmed down. Then she put him in her empty lunch box and stashed the box in her backpack.

"I guess the appointment's over, huh?" she said.

Dr. Gibbon didn't say a word. He pointed at the door.

In the waiting room, Rosemary put on her sweater. Mrs. Watson helped her put on her backpack.

"Don't forget your next appointment is in two weeks," she told Rosemary.

She gave Rosemary the old grouchy look.

"Don't keep Doctor waiting next time," she said.

Then she winked.

"And *don't* bring your rat."

# 9

# *Spot Wants Mousey!*

Rosemary jumped out of the car. She flung open the front door and raced inside. Spot toddled after her.

"Wo! Pay me!" he cried. He grabbed her leg.

"Not now, Spot!" she whispered.

She tried to pull him loose. She wanted to get to her room before Mom saw her.

"Rosie dear?" Too late. Mom came in, her arms full of papers. "I need you to set the table for dinner. I have a million things to do and a deadline in the morning."

She kissed the top of Rosemary's head.

"What's that funny smell? Have you been playing with the class rat again? Well, make sure you wash your hands."

She looked at Rosemary. "With *soap.*"

Rosemary nodded. Mom went into her office and shut the door.

"Gack," said Spot, his word for cracker.

"Later, Spot," she said. She needed to hide Cheese before he got loose again. And she didn't want Spot to see.

She ran upstairs.

*"Wo-o-o-o-o-o!"* Spot's angry wail followed her upstairs like a siren. Rosemary searched her room. There must be someplace to hide Cheese. *Pat-pat, thump. Pat-pat, thump.* Spot was coming up the stairs on his hands and knees.

She unzipped her backpack and opened her lunch box. Cheese looked all right. But he must be hungry. She put him on her shoulder.

How could she keep him safe from Spot?

On her desk was a vase filled with silk roses. She threw the flowers on the floor. She gently picked up Cheese and put him in the vase. She set a book on top so that he couldn't crawl out.

Cheese stood up on his hind legs. He pressed his paws against the glass.

*Bam! Bam! Bam!* Spot kicked her door.

"*Wo-o-o-o!*" he cried.

She flung the door open. Spot's face was red from yelling. Tears sprayed from his eyes. Spot was really, really mad.

Rosemary pulled him inside and slammed the door.

"Shhh!" she said.

She had to quiet him. Any minute, Mom would hear and come upstairs.

Rosemary pulled him onto her lap. She handed him a toy pony. Spot sucked on its tail. She rocked him, humming until he was calm.

She looked at the vase where Cheese was hidden. Oh no! Cheese lay on the bottom of the vase. His eyes were thin slits. His tongue was out. She stood up quickly, tumbling Spot to the floor.

"*Wo-o-o-o!*" he yelled.

Rosemary didn't care. She ran to the vase. She threw the book off the top. Cheese had no air! She'd forgotten air. He'd suffocated!

Cheese opened his eyes. Rosemary's knees turned to Jell-O. He wasn't dead! Cheese slowly stood up. He lifted up his head and sniffed.

Rosemary lifted Cheese out and cradled him against her cheek.

She caught sight of Spot in the mirror. His eyes were round.

"Mousey," he whispered. "Wo gots mousey. Me wants mousey, too. Mama!"

He headed for the door.

"No!" Rosemary sprang for the door and backed against it. "No, Spot. Don't tell Mama! Look, I'll share my mousey with you!"

She let Spot stroke Cheese.

Spot tried to grab Cheese. Rosemary pulled away. Spot's face turned red. His lower lip pushed out.

"Me wants mousey."

This was awful. Somehow she had to hide Cheese and think of a way to keep Spot quiet.

Her eyes darted around her room and finally landed on her toy stable. It had a hinged metal front. The cutout windows were crossed with bars. They were too small for a rat to climb through but big enough to let air in. She set Cheese carefully inside and shut the front. Cheese's nose poked out the window.

She fished in her bottom drawer for her stash of Christmas candy. There was a stale candy cane underneath her socks.

"Here, Spot," she coaxed. "Have this. Let's forget all about the mousey."

Spot reached for the candy. He sucked on it, smacking his lips. Rosemary went downstairs to set the table for dinner. Spot followed.

# 10

# *Spot Gots Mousey!*

"Wo!"

Rosemary struggled to wake up. Something tugged her blanket off.

"*Wo!*"

Spot was standing next to her bed, peering into her face. "Wo! Are you 'wake?" he asked.

It couldn't be morning already, could it? Rosemary squinted at her clock. It said 5:30 A.M.

"It's too early, Spot," she grumbled. "Go back to bed." She pulled the blanket over her face.

She could hear Spot padding around the room in his sleeper feet.

"Mousey!"

Rosemary woke up with a start. Spot must have seen Cheese!

She threw her blanket off again and sat up just in time to see Spot pad out of her room and down the hall.

"Wait! Stop!" she whispered as loudly as she dared. She couldn't risk waking Mom or Dad.

But Spot didn't even slow down.

Rosemary slid her feet into her slippers and grabbed her robe. She raced downstairs after Spot.

Spot could really move when he wanted to. Already he'd reached the foot of the stairs and was heading to the kitchen. "Mousey eat?" she heard him say.

Rosemary leaped downstairs. She skidded to a halt in the kitchen.

Spot teetered on a step stool. He gripped Cheese in his fist. Only Cheese's head showed. His black eyes blinked at her.

In his other hand, Spot held a cup of water.
"Mousey drink?" he asked. He tried to tip the
cup to Cheese's mouth, but the cup slipped.

*Splash!* Water poured over Cheese's head and
splashed on the floor. Startled, Spot dropped

Cheese. Cheese scurried away, shaking off water like a dog. He dashed under the counter.

Spot began to cry. He screwed up his eyes and his face got red. "Mousey gone!"

Rosemary dropped to her hands and knees. With Spot hollering like that, Dad would be downstairs any minute. She had to find Cheese first.

But Cheese was nowhere to be seen.

"What is going on in here?" Dad stood in the kitchen doorway. He blinked in the light. He looked funny without his glasses.

He squinted at the puddle of water.

"Do you two have any idea what time it is?" Dad's chin was scruffy with whiskers. He wore his old plaid bathrobe. His feet were bare, and his toes curled up off the cold kitchen floor.

"Sorry, Dad," Rosemary said. "Spot was hungry." She pulled a banana out of the fruit bowl.

"Well, you can go on back to bed now. I'll take care of Spot." Dad yawned. He picked up Spot and put him in his high chair.

"Mousey," grumbled Spot. But he took the banana Dad peeled.

Rosemary peered under the counter. There was no sign of Cheese. Where could he be?

"What are you doing?" asked Dad. "Go on back to bed. You can sleep for another hour." He yawned again. "Wish I could."

"Okay, just a minute," said Rosemary. She grabbed a towel to mop up the water. Cheese dropped out of the dish towel and landed on the floor. He sprinted across Dad's bare foot.

"*Yikes!*" cried Dad. He grabbed his foot and hopped up and down. "What was that?"

"Nothing," said Rosemary.

"Mousey," said Spot, his mouth full of banana.

"It felt like something alive," said Dad. "A mouse? Do we have mice?"

In horror, Rosemary watched Cheese dash across the floor. It must have scared him as much as Dad, she thought.

Luckily, without his glasses, Dad couldn't see Cheese. He took the dish towel Rosemary had dropped and mopped up the water.

"Maybe I'd better stop by the store after work and buy a mousetrap," Dad said. "Wouldn't want your Mom to find out we have mice!"

Dad picked up the coffeepot. Cheese was behind it. He stood up on his hind legs. His nose twitched. Dad didn't notice. He filled the pot at the sink.

While Dad was busy, Rosemary scooped up Cheese and slipped him into her bathrobe pocket. She cupped her hand over him. His whiskers tickled.

"Now," Dad said, "back to bed." He turned back to the counter and plugged in the pot.

"Okay, Dad, sure," Rosemary said.

She stopped in the doorway. Dad was watching the coffeepot and rubbing his chin.

Spot sat in his high chair. Banana was squished all over his face. He had banana in his hair. He waved a mushy piece of banana at her.

"Mousey," he said with satisfaction.

# 11

# *No Place for a Rat*

*Scritch. Scritch. Scritch-scratch.*

Rosemary dreamed she was lost in the desert.

*Scritch.*

Her throat was dry as sand. She was hot. She was cold. She was hungry.

*Scritch-scratch.*

Rosemary woke up. She yawned and opened her eyes. She must have fallen asleep after getting up with Spot.

She padded over to the toy stable and peered inside. Too dark. She turned on her bedroom light, blinking in the brightness.

Her throat still felt scratchy. Water. She'd forgotten to give Cheese water.

She took a plastic box of hair ribbons and dumped it out. Then she filled it from the bathroom tap.

Cheese drank greedily. His tiny tongue lapped up drops like a puppy. Then he sat up on his hind feet and cleaned his face with both paws. When he was done, Rosemary held out her hand, palm flat. Cheese ran up to her shoulder and ducked under her hair.

Rosemary looked at the mess inside her toy stable.

Rat droppings were everywhere, and the floor was wet. The toy saddle was knocked over. One plastic pony was chewed up.

Rosemary slumped down on the bed. She cradled Cheese against her cheek.

A toy stable was no place for a rat. In fact, her whole house was no place for a rat. Cheese needed a warm cage. He needed bedding that

could be kept clean, fresh water, and the right kind of food.

She realized she'd have to take Cheese back to school. It was best for Cheese. It was best for everyone.

But what about Brian? Before she could take Cheese back, she'd have to be sure Brian understood that Cheese was special.

She carefully set Cheese back in the toy stable and closed the door.

"It's just for a little while," she whispered.

She pulled on her clothes. She'd take him back to school that morning.

She bounded down the stairs to the kitchen. Her tummy rumbled. She was really hungry. Cheese was probably hungry, too. She'd take him some carrots for breakfast.

Spot sat in his high chair. He waved his spoon at Rosemary and grinned. "Mousey," he told her happily.

"Shhh!" she whispered, pressing her finger to her lips.

"Shhh!" answered Spot, pressing his finger to his lips, too.

✿   ✿   ✿

After breakfast, Rosemary ran upstairs. She needed something to carry Cheese in. Her backpack was too easy to escape from. And her lunch box would be full of food. Cheese would like that, but she wouldn't!

She dug in her closet. Clothes and shoes sailed out of her way. She rooted through her dresser. Underwear and socks went flying. She fished under her bed.

At last she surfaced with an old shoe box. It contained two dried-up cocoons and a few rocks. She dumped the mess onto her bed. She punched seven holes in the lid and slipped Cheese inside.

Perfect. He'd fit into her backpack, next to her lunch and the homework she'd forgotten to do last night.

"Rosemary! Megan's here! Time to go!"

"Coming, Mom!"

Rosemary stuffed the shoe box into her backpack. Then she swung her backpack over her shoulder and ran downstairs.

# 12

# *Rosemary and Cheese, Too*

"Rosemary, did you know Cheese disappeared?" said Megan.

Rosemary looked at Megan with wide eyes. Did Megan know? Did everybody know she had taken Cheese?

"Brian was supposed to take him home yesterday after school. But when his baby-sitter came to pick him up, Cheese was gone! Mr. Wilder said he must have escaped from his tank. Someone forgot to put the screen back on his tank, and *poof!* Out goes Cheese!"

Rosemary shook her head.

Megan was still talking. "I didn't think you knew. I saw you run out yesterday. Why didn't you wait for me?"

"I had an orthodontist appointment," said Rosemary.

At least that was true. She felt bad about not telling Megan the whole story. After all, Megan was her best friend. And maybe Megan could help her think of a plan.

She decided to tell Megan after all. She told her about the rat rescue, about Snookums and the big dog, and about Spot and what happened in Dr. Gibbon's office. By the time she was finished, they'd reached the school.

"What should I do now?" she wailed. "Cheese is inside my backpack. I want to put him back without anyone seeing him."

Megan shook her head. "Maybe I could distract the class somehow. You know, set off the fire alarm or something."

Rosemary giggled. "And when everyone runs out, I'll slip Cheese back in his tank."

Then she grew serious. "But we'd both be in real big trouble. I don't want to make things worse."

The buses arrived. Kids poured out into the playground. Brian whizzed by.

"Beggin' Megan!" he yelled. "Metal-mouth Rosie!"

He skidded to a stop and pushed his sunglasses up. He crossed his eyes and stuck out his tongue.

Rosemary rolled her eyes.

"Do you guys know if Cheese came back?" asked Brian. "Mr. Wilder said to leave his cage open overnight. He said rats have a great sense of smell. He said Cheese would be back inside his cage this morning, probably. Then I get to take him home for the weekend."

Rosemary blinked. Now she knew how to get Cheese back to his cage. But first she needed to be sure Brian would be a good rat keeper. She'd never let Cheese go with him if he couldn't be trusted.

"Brian, listen up."

She looked him straight in the eyes. She jammed one fist onto her hip.

"I'm holding you responsible for your treatment of Cheese." She made her voice sound like Mom's. She shook a finger right under Brian's nose.

"That rat better have a good time at your house or your name is mud, mister!"

"Geez," muttered Brian. He took a step back. "Who died and made you principal? 'Mud, mister, mud,'" he mimicked.

Then he grinned. "Mister Mud!" he shouted. "I like it! I really like it!" He ran off yelling, "They call me Mud! *Mister* Mud to you!"

"Do you think you can really get Cheese back into his tank?" asked Megan as they lined up. "Do you think Brian can be trusted to take good care of him?"

"I think so," said Rosemary.

While everyone else hurriedly hung up their coats and backpacks, Rosemary took her time. No one noticed when she took out the shoe box.

*Clap, clap, clap-clap-clap!*

Mr. Wilder called the class to the rug.

"Come join us, Rosemary," he called.

"Coming," she answered.

This was her only chance. While Mr. Wilder and the others were busy on the rug, Rosemary opened the shoe box.

"Go, Cheese," she whispered.

No one saw her lift him out and set him on the floor.

"Good-bye," she whispered. "Find your home."

Then she turned and walked to join the rest of the class.

She swallowed. Would Cheese find his way home? Had she done the right thing? She bit her lip.

Mr. Wilder was taking attendance. Please, please find your way home, she thought.

Rosemary closed her eyes to see better. In her imagination, she followed Cheese across the floor, up the table, and into his tank.

"Mr. Wilder!" It was Brian. He was coming back from the drinking fountain, taking the long way around, as usual.

"Mr. Wilder! It's Cheese! He's back! Just like you said!"

*Yes!* Rosemary heaved a great sigh. It had worked.

At lunchtime, Rosemary sat next to Megan.

"I told Mr. Wilder," she said, opening her lunch box.

"What did he say?" asked Megan.

Rosemary unwrapped her sandwich. "He said that taking things without permission is stealing. He said he was disappointed in me. He said he knew I wouldn't do it again." She looked at Megan. "And then he winked."

"I told you he was the nicest teacher," said Megan. She bit into her apple. "I'm glad Cheese is back. But now you don't have a pet."

"Oh," said Rosemary airily. "I've got a plan. If Brian can take Cheese home for the weekend, so can I. Mom just needs to meet Cheese face to face. Then she'll know how adorable he is. I'm sure she'll let me get my own rat as soon as I can pay for it."

She curled a piece of orange peel around her finger. "And I've got the name already picked out."

"What?"

Rosemary smiled. "Cheese, Too."

# Rosemary's Rat Care Tips

### Where to Get a Pet Rat

Rats are very clean, smart animals. Buy a rat from a pet store. Never try to trap a wild rat. Pet-store rats are free from disease; wild rats may not be.

Rosemary likes hooded rats, but black rats and white rats make good pets, too.

### Where to Keep a Pet Rat

Mr. Wilder's class keeps the rat in a glass aquarium tank. A dry one, of course! When they

bought it, they also bought a metal screen for the top so that Cheese couldn't climb out. Rats can gnaw through plastic, so a hamster cage is not a good idea. And the wire floor of a rabbit cage could injure rats' feet.

A glass aquarium tank is safe and easy to clean. When Rosemary wants to take Cheese home for the weekend, she takes the whole tank. If she had a tank at home, she could carry Cheese back and forth in a travel cage.

### What to Put in Your Rat's Cage

Molly, the pet-store clerk, told Mr. Wilder's class to use only pine or fir shavings. "Why not cedar shavings?" asked Brian.

"The oil in cedar shavings could irritate your rat's eyes," she told them. So they bought a big bag of fir shavings.

They bought a bag of food and a pottery dish to hold it. "No plastic!" reminded Molly. "Rats chew right through it." They also bought a water bottle to hang on the side of the aquarium.

Rosemary feels that all animals should have a private place, so she put in an empty tissue box as well. Cheese gnawed a hole in one side for a door. He likes to sleep inside. That way he can escape the noise and confusion of the busy classroom from time to time.

A glass tank can really heat up, so be sure to keep it out of the sunlight.

### How to Clean Your Rat's Cage

Rats need their cages cleaned often. Mr. Wilder's rat keepers do this job every week. One rat keeper holds Cheese while the other one empties the cage and puts in fresh bedding. Both rat keepers wash their hands afterward. Cheese also likes something to chew, so they put in cardboard tubes from empty rolls of toilet paper.

### What to Feed Your Rat

The rat keepers check Cheese's food and water every day. In addition to small-animal kibble the class buys at the pet store, Cheese enjoys scraps from lunches. But he is given only healthy foods such as fruits, vegetables, nuts, and seeds—never chocolate or salty or fatty foods.

Cheese likes to hide food in his bedding, so every morning the rat keepers pick out scraps of food he didn't eat the day before. They don't want rotting food to attract flies or make Cheese sick.

### How to Hold Your Rat

Rosemary insists her classmates pick up Cheese correctly. Never squeeze your rat or pull his tail. "And," she tells them, "be sure to wash your hands before you pick him up. If you smell like food, he might bite you!" Rats cannot see well, so they rely on their noses to tell them if something is good to eat.

When your hands are clean, very gently dangle them inside your rat's cage. Let your pet rat smell your fingers. Give your rat a carrot or other treat. If you do this every day from the time you first get your rat, your rat will learn your smell. Soon your rat will come to you.

Slide your fingers under your rat and lift him on your palm. Hold him close to your body so that he will feel safe. Rats like to sit up high. Your rat will enjoy sitting on your shoulder, behind your hair, or even on top of your head. Some rats can be trained to ride in pockets.

Keep your rat safe from danger: cats, dogs, and small children. Treat your rat with kindness and respect, and he will be a friendly, loving pet.